WALT DISNEY PRODUCTIONS
presents

Pluto the Detective

Random House  New York

Book Club Edition

Mickey and his dog, Pluto, lived together
in a cozy little house.
They were very good friends.

Every morning Pluto ran out to get
Mickey's paper.

Then they
played tug-of-war
with the newspaper.

Mickey always
let go first.
So Pluto always won.

Sometimes they played go-fetch.

Mickey threw a stick.

Pluto ran after the stick and brought it back to Mickey.

One day Mickey was reading the paper.
He saw something very interesting.
"Hey, Pluto," he said. "Listen to this."

"The paper says there was a big
jewel robbery yesterday!" Mickey said
excitedly. "Fifty thousand dollars'
worth of jewelry was stolen from Otto's
Jewelers. The owner is offering
a five-thousand-dollar reward
to anyone who helps find the jewels."

"I am sure the two of us could track down those robbers," said Mickey. "Help me find my detective outfit."

Mickey put on his detective
hat and coat.
Pluto put on his meanest look.

They went outside
and started searching.
Pluto sniffed everything
along the way.

He kept his nose close
to the ground so he
would not miss anything.

Then Pluto smelled
something and started
to run.
"Is it the robbers,
Pluto?" Mickey asked.

Pluto just
ran and ran.
He pulled Mickey
behind him.

Suddenly Pluto jumped over a fence—

and broke his leash.

Mickey fell flat on his face.

On the other side of the fence, Pluto found what he was looking for— a bone!

But just then Pluto saw Butch, the biggest, ugliest, meanest-looking bulldog Pluto had ever seen.

The bone lay on the grass close to Butch.

Luckily Butch was asleep.

Pluto knew he should not take the bone from Butch.

But the bone was too good to pass up.

Pluto picked up
the bone
very quietly.

Just then Butch opened one eye
and growled.

Off ran Pluto,
carrying the bone.

Butch followed close behind.
They ran down the street.
They turned a corner and
knocked over the grocer's
fruits and vegetables.

Pluto needed
a place to hide from Butch.

He saw a door and ran through it.
He was going into the Hall
of Mirrors!

Inside, Pluto was
surprised to see
a lot of dogs.

There were thin ones
and fat ones.
They were all
carrying bones.

Pluto
thought
it was very
strange.

Suddenly he saw
Butch.
Butch looked huge.
Pluto had to get
away from him.

HALL OF MIRRORS

TICKETS

See
yourself
as a
DWARF

Pluto ran out of
the Hall of Mirrors.

He was still holding
the bone.

Butch was chasing
him again.

Pluto almost ran
into a little girl
with a lollipop.
She dropped her
lollipop, and he
dropped the bone.
Butch picked
up the bone and
walked away.

Pluto did not stop running until
he came to the park.

Then he saw that Butch was not
chasing him.

He looked for a place to rest.

Pluto curled up under the park bench
and fell asleep.

Later, two men came into the park.

One was short and one was tall.

They were looking for something.

The short man pointed at the park bench.

"I hid the package of jewels under there," he said.

"You fool!" said the tall man. "It is probably gone by now."

The two men looked under the bench.

"There it is!" said the short man. "It is under that dog."

The package was wrapped in newspaper.
The tall man reached for it.
Just then Pluto woke up.

Pluto saw the man's hand on the package.

He growled.

The man tried to grab the package.

Pluto bit into it and would not let go.

Just then Mickey came into the park.
He was feeling sad and tired.
He had spent hours looking for Pluto.

Then Mickey heard something.
"That sounds like Pluto growling!" he said
to himself.

Mickey whistled for Pluto.

Pluto did not hear Mickey whistle.
He was trying to get the package
away from the two men.

Finally they lost
their hold and fell down.

Pluto trotted off with the package.
He was proud of himself.
All of a sudden he saw Mickey.

"Pluto!" cried Mickey happily.
Pluto ran to Mickey and licked him
on the face.

Then the two men ran up.

"That is OUR package," they said. "Give it to us."

"Okay," said Mickey.

The man grabbed the package from Mickey.
Then the string came loose.
Beautiful jewels began to tumble out.
"These must be the jewel thieves we were
looking for!" Mickey said to himself.

Mickey blew his whistle.

The robbers were so busy picking up
the jewels that they did not hear him.

Two policemen came running and grabbed
the thieves.

"Thanks, Mickey,"
said the policeman.
"You and Pluto
did a fine job."

The next night Mickey and
Pluto sat quietly by the fire.

Mickey had the five-thousand-dollar
reward.
Pluto had a fancy new collar and
a delicious new bone.

With thanks
for a fine
detective
job!
Town
Police